LEGO® CiTY

DETECTIVE CHASE MCCAIN: STOP THAT HEIST!

By Trey King

Illustrated by Kenny Kiernan

SCHOLASTIC INC.

ISBN 978-0-545-49596-7

LEGO, the LEGO logo, the Brick and Knob configurations and the Minifigure are trademarks of the LEGO Group. © 2013 The LEGO Group. Produced by Scholastic Inc. under license from the LEGO Group.

12 11 10 9 8 7 6 5 4 3 2 1   14 15 16 17 18 19/0

Designed by Angela Jun
Printed in Malaysia   106
First printing, January 2013

The LEGO® City Museum is having a costume party.

Everyone is coming to see the art and treasures. There is even a blue diamond!

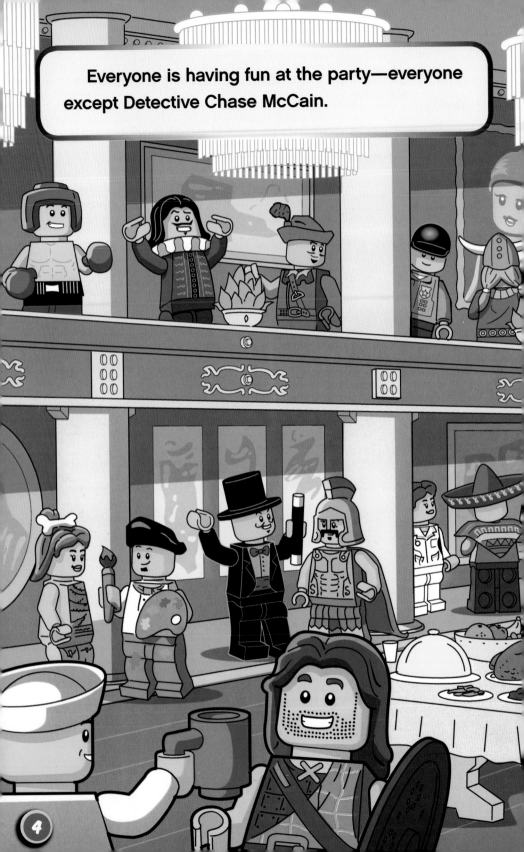

Everyone is having fun at the party—everyone except Detective Chase McCain.

Chase thinks a team of crooks will try to steal something tonight.
Where is Chase? He's in disguise!

Chase McCain is a master of disguise!
Before the party, he tried on several costumes to outsmart the crooks.

Circus clown?
Too funny.

Ocean King?
Too fishy.

Chase McCain is right—a team of crooks plans to rob the museum tonight.

But these are no ordinary crooks. Gregor, Greta, and Gary are the smartest crooks in LEGO City.

The crooks walk through the party before moving deeper into the museum.

The guests do not notice them, but Chase McCain knows that something does not seem right.

Enough eating. Let's go.

But I'm hungry!

Gregor, Greta, and Gary quietly sneak through the museum.

Dave is not as quiet.

Greedy Gary tries to escape with his own loot . . .

It's a car chase! Chase McCain follows the master thieves in hot pursuit on his motorcycle.